E'Moree T
BULLY PROOF KID

JOANNE F. BLAKE

Dedicated to

E'Moree AamIr Thompson

About the Author

Joanne F Blake is a poetess, writer, wife, mom, and Glam-Ma to 3 awesome boys. She lives is Augusta, Ga., home of The Godfather of Soul, James Brown. A professionally trained caregiver, Joanne began doodle writing as a teen while living in Europe. Today, she is a published poet in several anthologies by Train River Publishing and a writer of this new children's literature book.

One day while at the play-ground E'Moree wanted to slide. But a big kid pushed him down, he began to cry.

Kids were hiding behind trees, Pointing and laughing at E'Moree. But little did know he was a special B.P.

Bully Proof is what he is. He got up,

Looked around, and shouted 'stop

laughing at me, I'm not afraid big

bully!"

The Kids made a circle. The bully

Stepped inside. E'Moree said. "I will

Not fight you, lose your pride."

He said, "listen, I may be odd, cut from another tree, but that doesn't make you better than me."

.

The more E'Moree talked, the more
the bully forgot about being mean
All the kids were listening.

He told the bully, "If we fight it will be done and over, but we can be friends forever, BP friends."

One kid yelled, "hey what's it gonna be? Are you gonna punch out his lights or are you BP?"

19

E'Moree began to sing. I'm BP Bully Proof. I'm headed to the top. You can join me if you want to.

Suddenly the bully joined in and all the kids cheered and yelled BP wins.

The next time you face a bully tell him you're BP Proof and there's room on your crew.

The End

CPSIA information can be obtained
at www.ICGtesting.com
Printed in the USA
LVHW070428061021
699652LV00014B/935

9 781087 899763